SCHOLASTIC

SCHOLASTIC TM/® Scholastic Inc. PO#2013070

Welcome to the true story of my life as a reader.

The kid in this book is named Henley. But Henley is a version of me. When I was a kid, reading was my biggest challenge. It was the thing that scared me most, because it was such a struggle. In school, when we were asked to do what was called "round-robin" read alouds, my worst nightmare was listening to each student read, knowing my turn was coming. As the book's passage made its way toward me, my hands would get clammy and my armpits would sweat. Then my heart pounded like a nervous drum.

Nothing felt lonelier than being the kid in class who couldn't read well. Deep down inside, I knew I was as smart as everyone else. I also knew that I really liked stories and the pictures that go with them in some books.

Fortunately, through athletic scholarships and people who believed in me, I was able to go to college. That's where my reading struggles really showed themselves. Trips to the grocery store were stressful because there was so much reading involved in the simple act of buying food. I would misread labels and grab the wrong items. Once, I picked up apple*sauce* thinking it was apple *slices*. I didn't notice my mistake until I got home, realizing that it was my inability to understand the differences in the label wording that caused the mistake.

Mishaps like that kept happening. And they showed me that I needed to make an important decision. I wanted to be a better version of me, which meant becoming a stronger reader. I began by practicing reading as much as I practiced football. This meant working at reading just as hard as I worked at sports. The whole thing felt impossible at times. Thankfully, I was surrounded by many caring, patient adults who nurtured me into a reader, especially my mom, who, in my eyes, is a superstar. Mom and others helped me understand that there's no such thing as a "bad" reader. They showed me that my reading struggles weren't my fault and didn't make me a bad person. It's just the way my brain is wired. I sometimes have trouble with the words on the page.

This was all very important for me to come to believe — that I'm not good or bad because of how I read. I also figured out that comparing my way of reading to other people's is a waste of time. It's like comparing my name or my smile with someone else's. These are the things that make me who I am, and that make me special.

And it's why sharing *My Very Favorite Book In The Whole Wide World* with you is so important to me.

— Malcolm Mitchell

I was a grade-school graduate who later went to college, always in search of books that spoke to my heart.

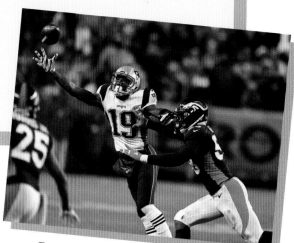

Even as a Super Bowl champ, I spent my free time off the field getting stronger at reading.

To my mom, my very favorite person in the whole wide world.
— Malcolm

To my lovely mother, Carmelinda, who always encouraged me
to read . . . and draw!
— Michael

Library of Congress Cataloging-in-Publication Data available
ISBN 978-1-338-22532-7
10 9 8 7 6 5 4 3 2 1   21 22 23 24 25
Printed in Malaysia 108 • First edition, January 2021
Book design by Doan Buu • The text type was set in Rockwell. The display type was set in Loyola Pro.
The illustrations were created digitally, using Photoshop with hand-done textures made with ink and pencil.

MY VERY FAVORITE BOOK IN THE WHOLE WIDE WORLD

by **Malcolm Mitchell**

illustrated by **Michael Robertson**

Orchard Books

An Imprint of Scholastic Inc. | New York

Hi! I'm Henley.

And this is a story about finding my very
favorite book in the whole wide world.

But it wasn't as easy as it sounds.

Reading can be hard, you know?

Once upon a time, everyone thought I hated to read,
but that's just not true.

In some books the words are too big, the sentences too long, and there are way too many pages.

In other books the pictures have zero to do with cool things I like, or with what's inside of me.

I do try, but some books are so giant, if I stood on them, I would turn into a GIANT!

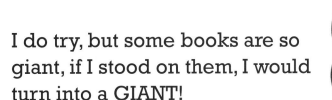

Other books are so boring, I'd rather use them as pillows.

When I'm supposed to be reading homework, I'd rather play football in the backyard.

When I'm asked to read the cookbook to help make dinner, I would rather see how many grapes I can fit into my mouth.

Once, I took a wagon full of books to the town swimming pool to find out how good they could swim.

When I tried to read books about dinosaurs, they made my brain hurt. So I gave the books back to the dinosaurs.

I've tried reading books about mountains, pickles, aliens, monsters, cats chasing mice, and mice chasing cats. I even found a book about cats chasing mice up a mountain while aliens eat pickles with monsters, but none of those made reading easier or more fun. But that all changed when Mrs. Joy gave the worst homework assignment ever.

"Find your very favorite book in the whole wide world and bring it to school tomorrow. It can be a book about anything. Just make sure you love it, because you'll be sharing it with the class."

The school bell sounded like a hundred horns blowing in my ear. Thinking about the yucky homework assignment gave me a super headache and made my hands sweaty.

On the way home from school, I stopped by the mighty library hoping to find any book that could be my very favorite.

My friends went into the library ahead of me. When it comes to finding books, I'm not so fast.

Inside, there was a nice man sitting behind a jumbo-sized desk. I asked him if he could help me find my very favorite book in the whole wide world.

He showed me books about science, and adventure, and squishy animals. He flipped through the pages of books about flags, farms, and holidays. He'd found plenty of books with twisty-big words, sentences as long as my legs, and pictures that tangled the pages. It gave me the heebie-jeebies.

When I saw my friends in the middle of the library, having fun and reading, I felt more lost than ever.

The next place I tried was Mrs. Rackley's Bookshop.
Maybe she could help me find my favorite book.

Mrs. Rackley did what she does best. She brought piles and piles of books. I looked and looked and looked, but I couldn't call any of them my very favorite book in the whole wide world! All those pages, and all those words, made my eyes tired. I realized it was going to take a book-miracle to find my very favorite book!

I grew a sad face and stomped all the way home.

Mama was unloading the dryer and she could tell I was having a crummy day.

I told her all about the worst-ever homework assignment.

"The librarian and Mrs. Rackley tried their best to help me find a book, but it was no use. I'll never find my very favorite book in the whole wide world!"

With a voice as warm as rolls from an oven, Mama said, "Henley, sometimes the best stories can be found inside ourselves." After a sweet kiss on the forehead, Mama's words lit up inside me.

"The librarian and Mrs. Rackley tried their best to help me find a book, but it was no use. I'll never find my very favorite book in the whole wide world!"

With a voice as warm as rolls from an oven, Mama said, "Henley, sometimes the best stories can be found inside ourselves." After a sweet kiss on the forehead, Mama's words lit up inside me.

"Everyone thinks I hate to read, but that's not true! Yes, some words are too big, and some sentences are too long, but that's not my biggest challenge. Before today, I just hadn't found a book I wanted to read. I hadn't found the words or pictures or pages or sentences or subjects that showed me, me."

That's when I had a brilliant idea!

The next morning, I could hardly wait for my turn to share my very favorite book in the whole wide world!

"So last night I wrote a book! It's called *My Very Favorite Book in the Whole Wide World*. It's about a big, fat, bumpy journey to finding the perfect book. My book has words and pictures and pages that show me, me. And that show *you* me."

When I started reading my book out loud for everyone to hear, I struggled. But soon my words began to flow. The pictures I drew danced off the pages. "Everyone can have a very favorite book in the whole wide world, even if they have to write it."

When I was done telling my story, all my classmates clapped and cheered.

My teacher gave me a gold star on my homework.
And that's the truth!